# BULLY on the BUS

KATHRYN APEL

First American Edition 2018
Kane Miller, A Division of EDC Publishing



First published in Australia 2014 by University of Queensland Press
Rights for this edition arranged through Australian Licensing Corporation
Design and illustrations by Jo Hunt



For information contact:
Kane Miller, A Division of EDC Publishing
PO Box 470663
Tulsa, OK 74147-0663
**www.kanemiller.com**
**www.edcpub.com**
**www.usbornebooksandmore.com**

Library of Congress Control Number: 2017958276

Printed and bound in the United States of America

1 2 3 4 5 6 7 8 9 10

ISBN: 978-1-61067-770-7

*To Mum, who knew how to "read" bullies.*

## The Bully

She's big.
She's smart.
She's mean.
She's the bully on the bus.
She picks on me and I don't like it.

But
I don't know
how to make her
stop.

## Bully Ways

Hurting hands

push,

pull,

poke,

prod,

pinch.

*Ouch!*

I wriggle and squirm,

move away –

but sly fingers

follow.

Sneaky feet

trip,

kick,

stomp.

*Eeeoooomph.*
Like a clumsy camel
I stagger … stumble …
sprawl flat on my face
as the bus crowd
claps and cheers.
But not Ruby
or me.

Most of all, the bully hurts me with her words.

They spew out
of her mouth like
lava from a volcano.
Red-hot, dangerous words,
burning right down, deep inside.

"Everybody knows, that Leroy picks his nose,"
the bully chants.
"Picker-Licker Leroy, he's the Booger-Boy."
And everyone laughs …
except Ruby
and me.

The bully is mean.

But
I don't know
how to make her
stop.

## Big Bully

The bully is
bigger than Ruby,
much bigger than me,
as big as my mom,
but not as big as Dad.

She doesn't go to our school –
goes to high school,
doesn't like school,
says it's stupid
and for dummies.

I like school!

Show and tell,
have a try,
words I know,
reading groups,
playing shops
with my friends –
Mrs. Wilson's
*Superkids*!

The bully says she's quitting school
and *never going back*!
She wants to be a hairdresser;
work full-time at the salon
where she works on weekends;
gets her hair done
for free.
She says, "Soon there'll be
no more school – ever!"

But until then she's
still
on
the
bus
with
me.

## Yes You

"DJ – stop teasing the little kids,"
the bus driver says.

"Who, me?"
she asks, as sweet and soft as cotton candy.
"I didn't do a thing."

She pulls my hair
then flicks my ear
and when I turn around she growls,
"Face the front.
I've seen enough of your
ugly face."

Sometimes the bully makes my eyes cry.

"Look at the baby,"
she says to the other kids.
"Crybaby Leroy – did you forget your pacifier?"

"Leave my brother alone,"
Ruby says.
"He's not hurting you."

"Shut up!"
snaps the bully
as she turns around to snarl
at Ruby
and her friends
three rows back.
"It's none of your
business, Roo-bee.
Little girls in grade five
shouldn't tell high school kids
what to do!"

Then she spins around,
jabs her finger
at me,
shakes her
shaggy orange mane
and roars,

“WHAT
ARE **YOU**
LOOKING
AT?”

## Bus Driver

Sometimes
in the afternoon,
when we wait for all the kids
to get out of school and on board,
the bus driver turns around
in his seat for a chat.

He's like my grandad –
not much hair on his head,
but it's in his ears and up his nose
instead.

The driver likes it when I tell him
what the *Superkids* have been learning.
"Mrs. Wilson's a good teacher," he says.
I tell him I know that!

Sometimes
the driver tells me about
when he was a boy,
and he rode
bareback to school

with his brothers and sister
on an old horse
called Youngen.

But when the bus door shuts
and the engine starts,
the driver switches off.

"I can't be chatting while I'm driving,"
he says, eyes on the road, as we start to roll.
"It's a big responsibility getting all you kids
home safe."

And he's back in his own world,
facing forward,
blocking out
bus kid noises
and I'm trapped.

Don't feel **safe**
going **home**
with the bully
on the bus.

## The Wheels on the Bus

*The wheels on the bus*
*go round and round*
*all the way to*
*home.*

"The Baby on the bus goes,
'Wah! Wah! Wah!'"
the bully bellows, pointing at me
as the bus crowd choruses the cries,
"Wah! Wah! Wah!"
louder and louder until
**"Wah! Wah! Wah!"**
The bus driver thunders,
**"Stop that racket!"**
and everyone screams laughing,
except Ruby
and me.

Blood thumps
loud and hot
in my chest,
                head,
                      ears,
and the wheels on the bus go
round and round
much
too
slow
for

me.

## Drop Offs

Bus stops

door opens

kids off

goodbye chorus.

Door closes

stories chopped

words flung

through windows.

Bus moves

pulls away

driving off

leaving kids

silent actors

miming words.

On the bus

faces pressed

to the glass

calling out,

"I can't *hear* you!"

And the driver
changing gears
doesn't hear,
doesn't want to,
in a world
of his own,
eyes the road
straight ahead.
Does his job.
Drives the bus.
Drops the kids
home safe.

# Into the Blue

I hunch down low
in my seat and watch
farms flick past.

Cows,
fences,
trees,
branches reaching high
to the sky,
birds flying
free.

I wish I could climb
to the top of the tallest tree
then step out into
the cool blue sky

and fly

away from the bully
words,
kids,
tears.

But I'm trapped
on the bus
in my seat
with the bully
right behind me –
bubbling,
boiling,
burning
to explode

at me.

## Our Stop

As the bus
rounds the bend I reach down
for my bag.

Almost home.

Grasp,
tug,
pull.
But it's stuck!

Bend over,
reach under,
pull harder,
still stuck.

Then I feel
something **heavy**
on top
squashing down.

Wriggle fingers
underneath,
try to free it.
    Presses harder.
Peering under
I see
        *big bully shoe*!

“Loser,” the bully hisses.

I pull.

## Free!

Tires
crunch gravel.
Door opens.
Bully shoe slips away.
I grab my bag and
stumble
  along the aisle,
    down the step,
      out the door.
Crunch gravel
underfoot,
guzzling great gulps of air.

Free!

No
bully ways,
bully words,
bully feet,
baby tears.

Just Ruby
and me
and a long, dusty track
stretching into
the weekend.

## Sticks and Stones

We
walk,
Ruby's ponytail
swishing as she marches ahead
kicking sticks
and stones
to clear a path
for
her anger.

I find a stick
on the side
of the track –
start to drag it,
weaving backward,
watching a long, skinny trail
snake out
behind me.

Swish,
      sweep,
            swerve.

"Leroy!

The weekend will be over
before we're even home,"
Ruby cries.
"Come on!"

I run,
scribble stick
skidding behind me,
while Ruby
waits
hands on hips,
scuffing shoes
and scowling.

"Are you mad at me?"

Ruby huffs.
"I'm not mad at *you*,"
she says,
picking up a stone
and hurling it across the field.

"But I'm sick of
the kids on the bus,
and DJ and her stupid, nasty names."

I hunch over,
start drawing
a circle
in the dirt
with my scribble stick.

Ruby stoops,
plops rocks
in place
for eyes,
then I scratch
a long sweeping arc of sadness
for the mouth.

"Dad says,
'Sticks and stones
may break my bones
        but names will never
        hurt me.'"

I toss my stick into
the grass,
slip my hand into Ruby's
and squeeze tight.

"But it's ***not*** true,
is it, Ruby?"

## Cupcake Critters

Saturday
is baking day.
"What will we make today?"
Mom asks.

I want to make
cupcakes so we can have
LOTS of cakes.

Ruby measures the flour and sugar.
Mom pours the milk.
I get the butter
and crack the egg
all over the counter.
We mix the mixture
then Mom and Ruby spoon it
into cupcake liners
while I spoon it into
my mouth.

"We can make cupcake critters,"
I say, while Ruby and I lick the bowl.

When the cupcakes cook
and cool
we mix colored icing and
use candy and sprinkles to make
crazy cupcake critters.

Dad is home
for lunch and wants
to help
eat
the icing,
the candy,
the sprinkles,
but we say,
"No! Go away."
And Mom says, "Look at you –
you're filthy. Go and wash your hands."

Then we
        giggle,
              gobble,
                    guzzle,
                        gulp

until all the leftover candy
is gone
in monster mouths.

Mom
shakes her head,
but she's laughing
when Dad comes back
sniffing around like a hungry wolf.

"Where is all the candy?" he growls,
grabbing Mom in his paws
as she squeals,
pointing at Ruby
pointing at me
looking guilty,
laughing out loud
looking at Dad
catching on
as he howls,
"You ate all the candy!
Little piggies."

Then he tickles our tummies
until we're one big breathless laugh,
and Mom cries,
"Stop it!
They'll laugh themselves sick
after all that sugar."

## Hungry Wolf

Dad is drooling and
licking his lips
over our crazy cupcake critters.
We help him pack his cooler
with the thermos, milk,
sugar, mug and tea bags,
and tell him he can choose
two cupcakes for afternoon tea.

"These'll keep the wolf at bay,"
Dad says, choosing the biggest,
stickiest cupcakes
on the rack.

"You can't take this one,"
I say, pointing at a green-eyed monster
cupcake with chocolate sprinkles,
white jelly bean teeth
and bright-green candy eyes.

"It's for Mrs. Wilson."

"Mrs. who?"

"You know … my teacher!"

"That's okay then," Dad says,
hoisting up his cooler and heading for the pickup.
"But make sure you leave the rest

*for me*."

"Next time I want to make one for
<u>all</u> the *Superkids*," I say.

"Good idea," Dad says.
"They can <u>all</u> share one – and the rest will be

*for me*!"

## Playing Pretend

"What are we going to play?"
I ask Ruby.

Our rooms are tidy,
jobs done.
Ruby practiced her
trumpet, loudly,
while I helped Mom clean up
the kitchen.
Dad is across the field
digging a new dam.
Ruby and I have all afternoon
to play.

"Let's pretend
I'm a bully."

I snort.

"You can't be
the bully, Ruby,
your hair's always brown.
The bully's hair is always
changing color."

"You'll just have to
use your imagination,"
Ruby says.
"Today it's brown,
but tomorrow,
it might change!
Now, pretend I'm the bully
and you have to make me
stop
bullying you."

I don't like that game.
Don't want to play.
Had forgotten
the bully.
Don't want to
remember.
But Ruby won't listen.

Starts to

poke,

prod,

push,

pull,

pinch.

"I don't like it
when you're a pest, Ruby,"
I grumble.
"Stop it now."

Ruby laughs,
takes my hat and
runs away
shrieking.
So I chase her,
leaping and bounding,
as kangaroos
scatter like skittles
and we run helter-skelter
screaming over the field

until I stop,
huffing and puffing.

"Give
me my
hat," I gasp,
"or you'll
have no one
to play with,
you big bully."

Ruby tosses my hat
and I catch it as she tackles me
gasping and giggling
into the grass.

"Next time *I'll* be the bully," I say.

But Ruby doesn't laugh.

"No way, Leroy.
Bullies aren't cool.
You be yourself.

You're
better than a bully
any day."

## Sick of the Bully

On Monday
I'm slow to get dressed.
My tummy burns
and churns
and I feel
sick.

Sick
of
the
bully.

"Hurry, Leroy," Mom says.
"The bus will be here soon
and you'll be running
down the track
to catch it."

*What will the bully do today?*

"I don't feel well.
Can I stay home?"

Mom frowns,
checks
my head,
my throat,
my eyes.

"You don't look sick.
I think you'll be all right.
Besides, you've got to take
Mrs. Wilson's cupcake critter,
don't forget."

"Maybe you should drive me,
so the green-eyed monster
doesn't get squashed."

"But the bus goes right past
our house," Mom says,
"and I don't need to
go to town today."

"The bus is noisy,
squishy-fishy,
rough 'n' tough
and takes so long.
I'd just like you
to take me."

But Mom doesn't understand.

"I think you had too much fun
playing with your big sister
on the weekend, but now it's time
for school again.
Go on the bus with Ruby,"
she says, "and I'll be waiting
to hear all about
your day."

Mom doesn't help.

## Seats

"Ruby,
sit with us
at the back,"
her friends call
as I slide into a seat,
in the middle of the bus, and
hug my schoolbag on my lap
with two cupcake critters
safely packed inside.
One for Mrs. Wilson
and one for
me.

Ruby smiles
as she passes, but is soon
crouched in a huddle
sharing a weekend's worth of secrets
with her friends.

## Hungry

The bully
is on the prowl
pacing the bus on the hunt
for food.

"Hey, Loser.
What did Mommy pack
for lunch today?"

I squirm
toward the window,
use my body as a shield
so my bag
is out
of
reach.

I don't want the bully
to find my
cupcakes.

"Leroy,
my little friend,"
the bully sings as she
slides into the seat
beside me, smirking
through a jagged curtain of
black hair.

"What's for lunch?"

## A Pinch ...

I look around
for Ruby,
the bus driver,
someone to help.

But all I see is
bully hair,
bully nails
and painted bully face leaning
closer and closer as
sneaky fingers
                    pinch.

*Youch!*

Like a snake she strikes.
          Grabs my schoolbag.

The zip buzzes like an angry bee
and my bag gapes open.
Then the bully starts rummaging through

flicking hat,
spelling book,
reader
and pencils
into the aisle.

Mrs. Wilson says
we have to take care
of our readers,
but the bus floor is dirty
and now the pages
are crumpled.

I feel the tears
burning my eyes,
slipping down
my cheeks
and choking my throat as I
huddle against the window –
hiding,
hoping.

Why can't Ruby see?

I sneak a peek
and spy Ruby and her friends
lost in laughter
leaving me

all
alone

with the bully.

## ... And a Punch

"Naw.
How cute!
Leroy the Loser
has a LION lunch box.
D'ya think that makes him brave?"

I gulp,
reach out and
try to take my lunch box,
but the bully
punches my hands away and
unzips my lion lunch box,
shaking all the containers until she finds ...

"Cupcakes.
My favorite.
And there's candy on them.
Aww, thanks, Leroy.
Looks like I won't
go hungry after all."

"Ru-by!" I cry
as the bully drops my lunch box,
spilling containers across the floor.
The bully slides out of my seat
and away,
taking my
cupcake critters
with her.

"Not the green-eyed monster!" I cry.
"It's for Mrs. Wilson.
I made it …

… *it's … my … favorite.*"

The bully stops,
looks at the kids
in the seats around me
and laughs.

Some of them laugh

with her,

others look away

but no one

tries

to stop her.

*Why won't they make her stop?*

"You couldn't bake this

if you tried, Loser,"

the bully sneers,

biting into

my monster cupcake and crunching

two wide-eyed green candies

and sweet chocolate sprinkles

in one greedy gobbling mouthful.

"Besides," she sputters,

spreading cake crumbs everywhere,

"we *all* know I brought these

from home,

don't we?"

Too late,
Ruby
pushes
past the bully,
knocks the cupcake critter
free
f
a
l
l
i
n
g.

Crumbly mess,
bus floor,
bully howls,
bully feet
grinding
Mrs. Wilson's
bitten,
broken

green-eyed monster
into
the
grit.

Ruby slides
into the seat
beside me.

"You can make Mrs. Wilson
another one … a better one,
and I'll help you
keep filthy hands
off it," she says,
glaring at the bully.

## Drive You Crazy

"Urgh! Gross!"
the bully yells,
spitting
out the window
spraying slobber streaks
across the glass.
"I've been eating
Picker-Licker Leroy's
***booger*** monster cake.
I … feel … sick," she wails,
clutching her tummy
and rolling around on the seat.

The bus slows
to collect
more kids and the driver
turns around.
He stands,
points at DJ
and snaps,

"Quit the noise!
You're driving me crazy
and you're old enough
to know better.

Start setting an example!"

Then he looks at the floor,
which looks worse
than Ruby's bedroom!

My
hat,
reader,
pencils,
lunch box and
cupcake
are all spewed across the floor.

"This bus is NOT a trash can,"
the driver says,
"and I *shouldn't* have to
clean up after *you kids*!"

Then he spies
DJ's slobber trail
streaking across the window.

His head reels back
and his eyes bulge as he bellows,
"Who's been
spitting on my windows, again?
If I ever catch you,
you'll be
washing *every* window of my bus!"

Then he sighs,
shakes his head
and shuffles back to his seat.

"No one gets off this bus
until you clean up this mess,"
he tosses over his shoulder
as the bus starts rolling again.

## Dumb and Stupid

"Hey, Leroy,"
the bully sneers,
as I'm huddled in my seat
heading home.
"What's

572

+ 326

– 254

x 98

?"

"We don't know that yet.
Mrs. Wilson hasn't
taught us."

The bully laughs
a rude snorting sound.
"Leroy's dumb!
He can't do the sum."

I feel the red-hot
lava spill out of the
bully's mouth and ooze
over my face
burning it
clumsy red.

I'm good at math.
Mrs. Wilson says so.
But the bully makes me feel
dumb.

## Threatened

"You're not *scared*
of a few little *numbers*
are you, Loser?"

"That's stupid," says Ruby.
"He's too young to know that stuff.
I bet ***you*** can't do the sum!"

The bully jerks around,
jagged black hair swishing
like a storm cloud across her face as
she snarls at Ruby,
"Does the crybaby
need his big sister
to hold his hand?"

Then the bully kicks
my schoolbag
into the aisle
and squashes
my
fingers

under her big bully
elbow,
pinning them
to the metal frame
of the seat in front of me.

She leans in closer
and I'm stuck!

"If you tell,
I'm gonna get you,"
she hisses,
spraying spit
like poison
over my
face.

## Not Telling

Ruby wants me
to tell
but
I
say,
"No.
Don't
tell."

What will the bully
do to me
if I
tell?

Ruby huffs her hair
out of her eyes and
spins around,
gripping my shoulders
and leaning closer.
"It's not right. It's not FAIR!
She's nothing but a big bully."

Ruby looks me straight in the eye.
"You've got to tell someone."

I can't look at Ruby.
I gaze past her
into the distance and hear
red-hot lava words whistling
around like a steamed-up kettle
inside my head.

"*... I'm gonna get you ... If you tell ... I'm gonna get you ... If you tell ...*"

"You don't have
to put up with this, Leroy,"
Ruby says, squeezing my shoulder.
"Mom will know what to do.
Mom can stop it!"

But my insides are
twisting, turning
and churning
into lumpy,
bumpy tangled
knots
and I'm scared.

*Too scared to tell.*

I don't look at Ruby
as I shake my head
and mumble,

"Please, Ruby,
please
don't
tell
anyone."

## Green-Eyed Monster

"Did you give Mrs. Wilson the cupcake?
What did she say?"

Blood thunders around inside
my head and
my tummy
flip-flops,
but I don't
look at Mom.

I want to roar like a lion
and stomp like a dinosaur,
but my heart is howling like a hyena as I pull
my uniform shirt over my head
and mumble,

"It got squashed on the bus
and I don't think Mrs. Wilson likes
green-eyed monster cupcakes
anyway."

I hunt around,
grab my home shirt and
tug it on.
Then I peep in the mirror
at my mousy hair
crackling with static electricity,
and Mom
watching,
waiting.

## Home Reader

"Mrs. Wilson says you've been quiet
today – not joining in at group time,"
Mom says, reading the comment
in my home-school journal.
"And there's a note here to take better care
of home readers, especially around food?"
Mom sounds puzzled
and I gulp,
swallowing
a sob.

"I don't know what that's about,"
Mom says. "We always take
good care of your readers."
Mom shakes her head,
then eyes the clock.
"I've got to go outside soon
and move some hoses
around the garden,
so we'd better get into
this book."

My eyes are heavy
and my lips won't smile
as I fumble to open the reader.

"I hope you're not getting sick," Mom says,
putting the book
on the table in front of us
and smoothing the hair from my eyes.
"Maybe this *Superkid* needs
a super-early night tonight."

## Graph to School

On Tuesday,
we make a transportation graph
showing how the *Superkids* came to school.

> 6 walked,
> 2 rode bikes,
> 8 came by car,
> 9 came by bus,
> 0 came by boat, train, plane or helicopter.

If Dad
had a helicopter
(his dream chopper)
he could drop me out at school
on his way to roundup
and there'd be:

> 8 came by bus, and
> 1 came by helicopter.

If.

Or if Mom could drive me
it would be:

> 8 came by bus, and
> 9 came by car.

I wish
I didn't ever
have to go on the school bus
again.

## Too Many Tears

On Wednesday,
the clock ticks
like a bomb as I walk
through the kitchen,
dragging my schoolbag
behind me.

"Mom, can I go to a
different school?"

Mom pauses,
knife poised, air sliced,
as our sandwiches lie uncut
on the chopping board.

"But you love
Mrs. Wilson's class –
don't you?"

"Mmmm ...
I just want to go
to a different school."

"What about all your friends?"
she asks.

I dip my head
and hunch my shoulders.
I'd miss the *Superkids.*
I'd miss my teacher too.
But I don't want to go
on the school bus.

My eyes burn
then fill with tears.
I don't want
to cry but
I can't stop.
Soon the bus
will be coming –
and the bully on the bus.
The bully will see me
crying
and she'll tease me
again,

call me Crybaby
again.
Make me cry
all over
again.

But the tears
keep
falling
until they are
all
that
I am.

## Keeping Mum

Mom wraps her arms around me
and makes soft noises as she
pats my shuddery-juddery back.

> "What are all these tears about?"
> she murmurs.

"N … n … n … oth … th … th … ing."

> "Are you worried about something?"

"Tell her, Leroy," Ruby breathes,
gripping my cold jellyfish hand.

> "Is something happening at school?"

Ruby squeezes.
I shake my head.

> "Is something happening on the bus?"

Ruby sucks in her breath – squeezes harder
but I shake my head again.

> "Leroy, I can't help you if
> I don't know what's hurting you."

I swallow,
take a shuddery breath,
open my mouth

and hear hot, hissing words howling in my head.

"Nothing's wrong," I hiccup.
"I don't want to go on the bus.
I just want to go to school."

Mom frowns.

Looks at me … at her watch …
down the track … at the bus …
driving past … up the road …
leaving us …

behind.

A smile wobbles across my lips
and my tummy goes swirly soft
like ice cream melting on a sunny day.

Mom sighs,
gives me one
last hug
and sighs again.

"If you're sure
there's nothing wrong
then I guess I'd better
get these lunches packed
and take you both
to school."

But her eyes are dark with worry,
watching
as we drive.

## No Bully

On Thursday,
the bully is
NOT on the bus!
NOT in the morning.
NOT in the afternoon.
NOT at <u>all</u>.

Maybe
she's left school;
works full-time
at the hairdresser's
where she works
on weekends.
Maybe
she's never coming
back on the bus
again!

In the afternoon,
I laugh as I get off the bus with Ruby.
I bounce along the track,
my schoolbag joggling

with excitement,
startling kookaburras
who chortle delight
in the gum trees.

But I'm not laughing when
the bully is back
on the bus the next
morning.

## Star Superkid

On Friday,
I get the class award
for student of the week.

"Because you always treat others
with respect," says Mrs. Wilson.
"You're a caring member of our class, Leroy.
You're a *Superkid*!"

I dip into the teacher's treasure box –
pull out a pack of glowing star stickers.
A whole pack of glowing stars!
I'm going to put them on my bedroom wall –
sleep under the stars
every night.

Ruby
sees me running,
stops to wait
and I show her my prize,
tell her she can have some too
and we're grinning as we

rush
to the bus
to get home
and get stuck
into stickers!

## Stolen Treasure

I put the stickers in my bag and
hug my bag like a secret,
one hand tucked inside
clutching my treasure
safe.

I look out the window,
try to hurry the bus
home so I can

*show Mom my glowing stickers*!

Maybe
we can put them up
before Dad comes home
so we can *surprise* him
with a starry night.

I peek into my schoolbag,
see my treasure and
start to count
the stars …

"Whatcha got, Loser?"
the bully demands,
looming over
the back of my seat.

I jump.
Jerk my hand and
send my glowing stickers
falling
    to
    the
    ground.

I drop to my knees and
try to hide them.

Too late!

The bully's hand shoots out.
She grabs my stickers.

"Isn't that nice?"
says the bully,

waving the pack above her head.
"There's one for everyone."

Ruby is wedged against the window.
She starts scrambling over legs and
schoolbags, yelling,
"You're a thief, DJ.
Give them back!"

I jump up and
try to snatch the stickers.
The bully flicks them
higher.

"Give them back!"
I shout, stretching,
jumping,
reaching.
"They're my stickers.
They're MINE!"

"SIT IN YOUR SEATS!"
the driver thunders,
glaring into the rearview mirror.

"If I have to stop this bus
then you're all
going to see the principal
first thing Monday morning."

"Yeah, sit down, Crybaby,"
the bully taunts,
giving me a shove.

I fall into my seat and
see Ruby hovering
on the edge of her row
as the bully swaggers up the aisle
and back to her friends.
Then the bully
rips into my glowing star stickers.
She holds the sheets out the window
and lets them all

fly
away.

## Stuck for Words

"Leroy got student of the week today,"
Ruby says.

Mom puts my dinner on the table.
"That's great, Leroy.
Why didn't you tell us?"

"I forgot,"
I mutter,
not looking at anyone.

"Did you dip into the treasure box?"

I nod.
Mom waits.

"Well, what did you get?"

I don't answer.
My nose is prickling and
I blink hard.

"Leroy?" Mom asks.
"Where's your treasure?"

Tears rush to my eyes.
I tuck my chin tight into
my chest so no one sees them
run down my cheeks and
drip into my dinner.

"Gone," I mumble.

Dad clears his throat.
I know what that means,
but my mouth is thick
with sadness
and I can't
make the words
come out
into the room.

"Leroy?"

Dad's waiting,
but I still can't talk
past the big lump
that's blocking
all the words.

"He got glowing stickers,"
Ruby says.
"A whole pack of them."

"That's great!" says Mom.
"After dinner we can find
a special place to put them."

## No More Stickers

"NO!"

I drop my knife and fork
so that they clatter onto my plate
and flick bright-green peas
across the table.
"We won't put the stickers
anywhere.
There are
NO MORE STICKERS!"

The room echoes
with a quiet
so loud it
booms inside
my head,
my tummy,
my heart
until,

"That's enough."
Dad growls.
He stabs his pointer finger
at my bedroom door.
"Go to time out – now!"

But before I can move, Ruby grabs me.

"Leroy hasn't got the stickers,"
she says, scowling at Mom and Dad.
"DJ took them
and threw them all
away.
She's just plain nasty and
I don't like her."

Mom looks at Dad.
Then she looks at Ruby
and me.
"Who's DJ?"
Mom asks.

Ruby opens her mouth,
closes it again –
looks at me
and waits.

She looks right inside me
to the sad and scary places
where the bully burns me
with her red-hot lava words.

Ruby doesn't say anything.

Mom and Dad are watching.
They are quiet
and still –
waiting.

Everyone is waiting …

"Leroy,"
Dad says softly,
"who's DJ?"

My chest shivers as I take a long, jagged breath.

“She’s the bully on the bus,”
I say, and I feel
my words grow stronger.
“She picks on me and *I don’t like it.*”

## Words

No one wants to
eat dinner anymore.
We are full
of sadness.

Ruby
is fighting mad
and overflowing
with words –
telling Mom and Dad
*everything* the bully on the bus
has ever done
to me …
to her.

Dad listens,
face setting solid
like it's carved in clay
from the new dam.

Mom
keeps asking
questions.
She looks sad
and a little
bit angry.

I
mostly listen,
but sometimes words
jump out of my mouth
without me even
telling them to.
Words that make
Mom's eyes sadder
and make me feel
sick and
soggy
inside.

"She calls me Loser … and Crybaby … took my stickers … ate Mrs. Wilson's green-eyed monster … everybody laughs … nobody is my friend on the bus … no one listens … no one helps …

except Ruby.

*Why don't they make the bully stop?*

She said that she will *get me*
if I tell," I whisper.

"I didn't know,"
Mom says,
pressing kisses on my head
as she cuddles me close.
"I
just
didn't
know
what
was
wrong."

Dad is like a sleepy bear
waking up from hibernation
as he grabs Ruby and me
in a gruff and clumsy
squishy hug.

"You're good kids,"
he says, scruffing our heads
with his leathery hands.
"Good, *brave* kids."

All night Mom watches me –
gives me hugs
and wonky smiles,
and squeezes extra tight
when she says
good night.

It's like she's trying to
swallow the sadness
with all her
love.

I wish I could forget
the sad and scary places
the bully has made
inside me.

I wish I didn't have to
go on the bus
ever again.

I wish there never even *was* a bully.

I wish.

## The Dragon

Telling Mom and Dad makes
me feel worse
but better too.

It's a bit
like having a
fiery dragon
that you *think*
is inside your bedroom
but you don't *know*
until you open the door
and the dragon escapes,
and you can't catch it
and you don't know what
terrible things it's going to do.

But now *everybody*
knows there's a
dragon and it's
not your secret
anymore.

## Drive to School

On Monday
we drive to school,
Mom, Dad, Ruby and me.

"I thought you were doing
cattle work today," I say.

Dad winks.

"Gotta take care of this bully on the bus, first,
then I'll do the cattle work.
What do you reckon?"

I grin.

I'm jittery-nervous
and my insides are skittering around
like the cat after it woke up next to
a carpet snake,
but I feel brave and strong
and I'm glad I told.

I don't want DJ hurting me anymore.

At school
I snag Dad's hand and
lead the way to
the *Superkids'* classroom.

"Now you get to meet
Mrs. Wilson," I tell him.

## I Can Do It

Mrs. Wilson says,
**"Bullies only THINK they're tough."**

She helps me make a list
of things that **I** can do
to stop the bully on the bus.

Some things are
silly
and funny,
and we giggle
as we write them down.

I feel
BIGGER
and **stronger.**

When we're finished
Mrs. Wilson smiles widely,
her lips glossy red
around bright-white teeth.

"We are always here to help, Leroy,
and we *can* stop this," she says,
handing me a large, flat package.
"But I've got a hunch that
you will sort this out *yourself.*
Now, remember …"

## How to Bust a Bully

- Sit somewhere safe.

  Near the driver.

  Away from the bully.

- Ignore them.

  Tell yourself:

  ***I** don't care what you say.*

  ***I** don't want to be like you.*

- Get lost

  in a game, a book,

  a puzzle, a friend,

  a view.

- Throw a catchy comeback.

  *What's your beef, Bully?*

  *Bellow louder, I can't hear you.*

- Show and tell.

  ***Show*** the bully you don't care.

  ***Tell*** an adult.

- Find a *Secret Weapon.*

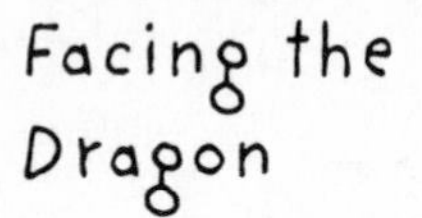

Mrs. Wilson helps me get organized
and out of the room so I'm the
first primary student
on the bus.

I take a seat away from
the bully and
sit close
to the front,
near the
driver's seat,
then wait for the bus
to fill.

Ruby grins
as she walks by,
sits with her friends
chattering like magpies
in the seats
behind me.

I don't look at the bully,
ignore her and
put my schoolbag
on the seat
beside me,
then look out the window
and get lost in thoughts about …

my *Secret Weapon*!

## Home Safe

The driver gets up
and sits in the empty seat beside me
for a chat while we wait.

"My friend Mrs. Wilson
says you're not just a *Superkid,*"
he says, scratching his head
so that his gray fuzz sticks out all crazy.
"She says you're a *Super-Special-Superkid.*
That you've even got," he winks,
then whispers, "a *Secret Weapon.*
But she assures me it won't hurt anyone."

He pauses, scratches his head some more,
making his hair look like dry grass that
chickens have been scratching at,
then he looks at me,
            looks at Ruby too.

“Remember, it’s my job
to get you home safe,” he says.
“You let me know if you need any help …
with that *Secret Weapon.*”

## The Secret Weapon

I put my hand on my bag,
feel the shape of my
*Secret Weapon.*
It takes up most of the space
and it's very heavy –
like pirate's
treasure.

"Whatcha got today, Loser?"
the bully calls
from the back of
the bus.

I squirm inside
but don't look,
don't answer,
don't huddle,
just think about
my *Secret Weapon.*

"Everybody knows, that Leroy picks his nose."

My face burns
but I
don't look,
  tell myself:
    *I don't care what you say.*
      *I don't want to be like you.*

*Bullies aren't cool.*
*Bullies only think they're tough.*

The driver's eyes
are watching in the rearview mirror
and I take a deep breath,
then very carefully
slide the *Secret Weapon*
out of my bag.

## The Big Bad Book of Fairy Tales

Mrs. Wilson says
there are secret messages
in this book,
but I have to read it very carefully
and look closely at all
the pictures.
She says it's important
not to rush
or I might miss the
hidden clues.

"Los-er Le-roy lost in spa-ace,"
the bully chants, her voice coming closer,
until she pauses
near my seat –
but I don't look up.
I hear Ruby whispering behind me and
I take slow breaths
and remember
the fiery dragon.

It’s not my secret
anymore.

Very slowly, I open the book.

Feel hot breath on my neck …

“DJ. You have a seat,”
the driver calls.
“Use it!”

Head down
I sneak a glance sideways and
see DJ’s body straighten
then slowly turn.
My hat topples
off my head
onto the seat beside me
and the bully struts
back down the aisle
to her seat.

I breathe.

## Little Pig

I start at the beginning,
at the very first story,
because I don't want to miss
any of the clues.
*The Three Little Pigs …*

I wonder if they're hiding
a secret message.
Where would it be?
Inside the mother pig's house?
What a mess! It looks like …
a pigsty.
There are so many places
to hide
a secret.

Ruby and her friends
peep around the side of
my seat, giggling,
but I'm too busy

to play their games.
Looking for hidden clues
is hard work.

*Once upon a time …*

## Lost in the Book

*Then I'll huff . . .*
*and I'll puff . . .*
*and I'll blow your house down.*

"Come on, Leroy. Time to get off."

I blink.
The big bad wolf
disappears. My sister is
waiting beside my seat
and Mom's standing
at the bus stop.
We're home
already?

I slide Mrs. Wilson's book
into my bag
and get off the bus
with Ruby.

"How was your day?" Mom asks.

"Good."

"And the bus?"

"Mmmm."
I'm busy thinking
about Mrs. Wilson's
hidden clues.

"Mom,"
I say,
"did Mrs. Wilson tell you
what secret messages are
in this book?
I can't find them."

Mom smiles and shakes her head.
"I think they're for you to find, Leroy.
You'll just have to keep looking."

Ruby laughs.
"Leroy is looking so hard
he'll end up falling *in* the book."

## It's All Just an Act

"Let's play *The Three Little Pigs,*"
I say. "You can be the little pigs,
and I'll be the big bad wolf."

Ruby raises her eyebrows,
looks at me,
grins.
"Have you
fallen into
*The Big Bad Book*
*of Fairy Tales*
already?"
she asks.

(Sometimes Ruby says the silliest things.)

We collect straw from the hay shed
and build a house
of straw.
It doesn't look
very strong!

Then we walk
over the field,
pick up sticks,
tie them together
with baling twine
and make a house of
sticks.

Next, we paint
cardboard boxes
to make a
brick house with a
bright-yellow door
and blue windows.
Little boxes
make the chimney
on top.

At last we're ready for
the wolf.
I rummage in my bedroom for
the mask.

What a long pointed nose it has.
What sharp white teeth it has.
What a lolling red tongue it has.
It looks
hungry,
fierce,
and mean.
It looks
just right for
me!

"I'm not your little brother anymore,"
I warn Ruby, as I slide the mask
over my head.
I growl in a gruff, tough voice,
"I'm the big bad wolf.
And I'll huff …
and I'll puff …
and I'll blow your house down!"

## Con-cen-trat-ing

All week I
go to school,
come home from school,
travel on the bus,
sit toward
the front –
away from
the bully.
She calls to me
but I don't
turn around,
don't listen,
don't answer.
I'm con-cen-trat-ing.

I hunt
and hunt through
*The Big Bad Book of Fairy Tales,*
but I can't find
the hidden messages.

Mrs. Wilson isn't giving any clues.
"Keep looking,"
she says, with a secret smile.
"You're getting closer."

## Little Red Robin Hood Comes to Play

"Let's play *Little Red Riding Hood,*"
says Ruby, "and *I* will be the wolf."

"But who will be Little Red Riding Hood?"
I ask. "She's a girl!"

"Not this time," says Ruby.
"Today *he* is wearing
red shorts and a
red riding hood."

"And he carries a
bow and arrow,"
I cry, "like Little Red *Robin* Hood."

Ruby laughs.
"Great idea, Leroy.
Now, what else
will we need?"

I get my red hoodie,
my bow and suction-cup arrows,
and my quiver 'cause I don't
want to carry a *basket*
full of goodies!

Little Red Robin Hood is ready.

## One Seat Away

On Thursday afternoon,
I'm late for the bus.
There is only one spare seat,
right in front of
the bully
with her flaming
bright-red
hair.

I sit,
open my bag and
get out Mrs. Wilson's book.

*Little Red Riding Hood* –
I was right at the good bit
when we got to school that morning.

The wolf had gobbled Granny,
and Little Red Riding Hood
was knocking
at
the
door.

*Little Red Riding Hood*
*skipped into Grandma's bedroom.*
*"Grandmother,*
*what big eyes you have."*

A crumpled
ball of paper
flies over my shoulder and
lands on Grandma's bed.
*Pffft!*
I tilt the book,
keep reading
as the trash rolls away.

*"Grandmother,*
*what a big nose you have."*

"Hey, Picker-Licker Leroy.
Get your nose
out of that book.
I'm talking to you."

*"Grandmother,*
*what big ears you have."*

The bully
flicks my ear.
It stings like
a green ant bite
and I don't like it.

***I don't like it!***

## Bully for YOU!

I know just what
Little Red Robin Hood would do …
I know just what ***I*** will do!

I turn around in my seat,
look the bully in the eye
and roar,

### "DJ, what a big bully mouth you have. And what big bully teeth you have."

Then,
biting off each word
like a snarling big bad wolf,
I growl,
"If
you
don't
leave
me
alone

then I'll huff

and I'll puff

and I'll blow

*all my germs* in your

big bully face!"

## Meltdown

DJ seems to
freeze in place as
her gaze darts
left, right,
down,
away,
and her mouth
gulps words
that are frozen
in her throat.

Then she shrinks
like a puddle of lava
oozing into
the seat
as the bus crowd
watches
… waits
and whispers.

DJ doesn't say
anything,
doesn't look at
anyone,
won't even look at
*me.*

She is as red as Little Red Riding Hood's cape.

I snarl my biggest,
toughest,
toothiest,

**"Grrrrrrrrrr,"**

then turn around
and sit down.

## Free to be ...

Ruby sits
in the row
opposite.
She sticks her thumbs up
and flashes
a grin.
The bus driver
watches me
through the mirror.
His eyes are smiling,
but he doesn't say
anything.
He just nods his head
and keeps
driving.

I take a deep breath
and smile.

Now it's time
to rescue
Little Red Riding Hood
and Grandma
from the big bad
wolf.

## Clued In

On Friday afternoon,
DJ is sitting
near the front of the bus
talking with the driver.

The driver sees me,
winks,
and asks if I've found
the secret messages
in Mrs. Wilson's book.

I look at DJ
but she's busy
fiddling with her shiny black
fingernails.

"I've nearly finished looking
through the *whole* book,"
I tell the driver, shaking my head,
"but I haven't found a single clue!"

DJ eyes my *Secret Weapon*,
clears her throat
and looks
at me.

"You must be pretty smart
if you can read that book
all
by
yourself."

DJ's voice is different,
like she's
finding new words
and trying to make them fit
in her mouth.

I shrug.

"I don't know all the words.
Just the stories. And the pictures.
That's how I read it."

DJ doesn't laugh,
call me dumb
or make me cry.

At first

she doesn't say anything –
just nods,
pauses,
then moves over
on the seat
so there's space
beside her.

DJ looks at the bus driver.

He's smiling.

"So …
Ummm …
Maybe I could help you …" DJ says.

*She's looking at me.*

## Super-Special Cupcake Critters

Saturday
is baking day.
"What will we make today?"
Mom asks.

I want to make LOTS of
cupcakes so we can have:
one for Mrs. Wilson,
one EACH for all the *Superkids*,
some for Ruby and me,
some for Mom
AND some for Dad, too.

Mom says we'll be baking all day
to make enough cupcakes.

"And I have to make the green-eyed monster.
With chocolate sprinkles, white jelly bean teeth,
and bright-green candy eyes,
for Mrs. Wilson."

Mom and Ruby don't answer.
They look at me and
try to smile.
Mom's eyes are
shining
tears

and I think we're all
remembering …

But then ***I*** remember
yesterday.
DJ
clumsy,
helping,
not nasty
but trying
to be nice.

"And I want to make one for DJ, too,
because I think she really does like
my cupcake critters," I say.
"But I don't know what
to use for the
hair."

# Acknowledgments

*Bully on the Bus* is very much a product of the writer's support network, from critter-buddies, to festivals, editors, and family.

I particularly acknowledge the support of: Curtis Coast Literary Carnivale, CYA Conference, and Bundaberg WriteFest who, through workshops, competitions, editorial opportunities, and valuable networking, have contributed to the development of this story.

There have been many critter-friends who've encouraged me and provided feedback – but particular thanks to Susan, who helped me see that Leroy's story wasn't the chapter book I'd written, but the verse novel I'd been longing to write.

I'm especially grateful to the wonderfully supportive team at UQP, particularly Kristina and Michele, who have both been such fun to work with. A joy!

Heartfelt thanks to my mum, whose constantly changing box of *Archie, Phantom* and all other comic books tamed the bullies on my bus, filling many hours of travel time, and sparking the resolution of Leroy's story.

My family continue to inspire and endure my writing endeavors. I've learned much about writing from my sons, and cherish our literary discussions – and shared Month of Poetry each January.

Sometimes as kids (and even as adults), we don't understand how our actions stress and distress others. I praise all the brave Rubies who try to put a stop to bullying. And I commend the bullies who are big enough to apologize, and then choose to make a positive impact.

Kathryn Apel is a born-and-bred farm girl who's scared of cows. She lives with her husband and two sons, among the gum trees, cattle and kangaroos, on a grazing property in Australia. There are also guinea pigs – and a Jack Russell that dotes on all the cuteness.